Superphonics *Storybooks* will help your child to learn to read using Ruth Miskin's highly effective phonic method. Each story is fun to read and has been carefully written to include particular sounds and spellings.

The Storybooks are graded so your child can progress with confidence from easy words to harder ones. There are four levels - Blue (the easiest), Green, Purple and Turquoise (the hardest). Each level is linked to one of the core *Superphonics® Books*.

ISBN: 978 0 340 79896 6

Text copyright © 2001 Clive Gifford
Illustrations copyright © 2001 Jacqueline East

Editorial by Gill Munton
Design by Sarah Borny

The rights of Clive Gifford and Jacqueline East to be identified as the author and illustrator of this Work have been asserted by them in accordance with the Copyright, Designs and Patents Act 1988.

First published in Great Britain 2001

10 9 8 7 6 5 4 3

First published in 2001 by Hodder Children's Books,
a division of Hachette Children's Books,
338 Euston Road, London NW1 3BH
An Hachette UK Company. www.hachette.co.uk

Printed and bound in China by WKT Company Ltd.

A CIP record is registered by and held at the British Library.

Target words

This Purple Storybook focuses on the following sounds:

igh as in **fight**
i-e as in **white**

These target words are featured in the book:

fight	alive	life	slime
fighting	arrived	like	smiled
Highness	beehive	mice	spike
Knight	bike	Mike	spine
knights	cried	mine	spiteful
might	crime	nice	spitefully
mighty	decide	nine	strides
night	dice	pies	swipe
right	die	pride	surprise
sighed	five	replied	tile
sight	hide	shiny	time
thighs	ice	side	tried
tonight	insides	Sire	twice
	knife	slice	untied

Vile	vines	whined	wife
Vileness	viper	white	wine

(Words containing sounds and spellings practised in the Blue and Green Storybooks and the other Purple Storybooks have been used in the story, too.)

Other words

Also included are some common words (e.g. **could**, **there**) which your child will be learning in his or her first few years at school.

A few other words have been used to help the story to flow.

Reading the book

1 Make sure you and your child are sitting in a quiet, comfortable place.

2 Tell him or her a little about the story, without giving too much away:

The spiteful Baron Vile is plotting to be King, so the White Knight is sent to fight him - with some little helpers!

This will give your child a mental picture; having a context for a story makes it easier to read the words.

3 Read the target words (above) together. This will mean that you can both enjoy the story without having to spend too much time working out the words. Help your child to sound out each word (e.g. **f-igh-t**) before saying the whole word.

4 Let your child read the story aloud. Help him or her with any difficult words and discuss the story as you go along. Stop now and again to ask your child to predict what will happen next. This will help you to see whether he or she has understood what has happened so far.

Above all, enjoy the story, and praise your child's reading!

Ruth Miskin's

Superphonics®
Purple Storybook

White Knight

by Clive Gifford

Illustrated by Jacqueline East

Hodder
Children's
Books

a division of Hachette Children's Books

King Mike and Queen Matilda
were sitting in their garden.

Suddenly, there was a rustling
in the bushes.

It was the beastly Baron Vile!

He knocked King Mike to the ground.

Then he grabbed Queen Matilda
and dragged her up on to his horse.

"Take your hands off my wife!"
cried King Mike.

"Who's going to make me?"
Baron Vile replied.
"You're too old and fat to fight!"

"Read this, old man.

You have until nine o'clock tonight

to decide!"

With that, Baron Vile rode out of sight.

King Mike went white as he read
the message:

Make me king,
or die in my
slime!
Love and hugs
Baron Vile
xxx

"N - n - no, not the slime!" he cried.
"Please, not the slime!"

King Mike called a meeting.

"What am I going to do
about the beastly Baron Vile?
He's hijacked my wife, and now
he wants to be King!

If I don't agree, he will make me
die in his vile slime!
I will be turned to stone in no time!"

"What about the knights
of the round table, Sire?"
asked the Slime Minister.
"Can't they fight him for you?"

"Oh, they've all resigned!"
sighed King Mike.
"They even took the table with them."

"Well, why not send for the White Knight,
Your Highness?" smiled a shy pageboy.
"He beat the viper with five heads
AND the spiteful one-eyed troll."

So King Mike sent for the White Knight.

"I'm fed up with fighting,"
said the White Knight.
"It's time for me to give it up,
Your Highness."

"Give it up?" said King Mike in surprise.
"But you're only nine!"

"I'm ten, Your Highness,"
replied the White Knight with pride.
"But I'm not very good at being a knight."

"You beat the viper with five heads,"
said King Mike.

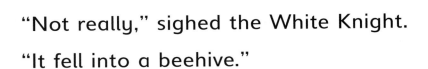

"Not really," sighed the White Knight.
"It fell into a beehive."

"Well, what about the spiteful
one-eyed troll?"

"I had a slice of luck there,"
said the White Knight.
"Just as we were about to fight,
a fly flew into the troll's eye."

"But you've got to help me!"
cried King Mike.
"Baron Vile is coming this very night!"
"If I don't hand him my crown,
I will die in his vile slime!"

"I could give it a try,"
sighed the White Knight.
"But I don't have a horse.
Can I borrow your bike?"

The shy pageboy helped the White Knight on to King Mike's bike.

"Do you want to take my white mice for luck?" he smiled.

"If you like!" replied the White Knight, checking the tyres.

The palace clock struck nine.

Baron Vile had arrived
with Queen Matilda (and a vat of slime).

"Soon, all this will be mine," he cried.

Baron Vile charged,

swinging his shiny spike.

The White Knight ducked,

and rushed to Queen Matilda's side.

Quick as a flash, he untied her,

and cried, "Now run and hide!"

"You should have done the same!"
grinned Baron Vile.
"I'll slice you with my mighty sword,
and then I'll dice you with my knife!"

The White Knight felt a chill
run up and down his spine.

"Can't we just talk this over,
Your Vileness?
I'd quite like a chat,"
said the White Knight.
His insides felt like jelly.

Baron Vile smiled spitefully,
and swung his spike.

"Oooh!" whined the White Knight.
"That's not very nice."

He swung his sword with all his might,
but it smashed to bits against
Baron Vile's chest.

"Let me show you how to fight,"
said Baron Vile.

With a swipe of his hand,
he knocked the White Knight
right off the bike.

The White Knight tried to hide,
but Baron Vile soon spotted him
in the vines.

"Oh, why can't I have a real fight?"
he sighed, with another mighty swipe.

"I think I'm still alive,"
said the White Knight,
rubbing his painful thighs.
"I'll try to climb over the wall."

But he slipped on a loose tile,
and his chain mail got caught on a spike.

He was stuck.

"What bad luck!" he sighed.

"And I did so like being alive!

I knew I should have given up fighting!"

Baron Vile was upon him
in five long strides.

He pulled off the White Knight's helmet ...

and out fell two white mice!

Baron Vile's face was white.

"N – n – no, not mice!" he cried.
"Please, not mice!"

He tried to hide behind a barrel of wine.

The White Knight stuck out his foot ...
and Baron Vile fell straight
into the vat of slime!

King Mike helped the White Knight
down from the spike.

Queen Matilda kissed him twice
on each cheek.

"That's the end of Baron Vile
and his life of crime!" cried King Mike.
"Now, boy, fetch that wine!
And bring pies, and ice cream!
It's party time!"